ALBANY COUNTY
PUBLIC LIBRARY
Serving the Laramie Plains since 1887

Laramie, Wyoming 82070

PRESENTED BY

A Friend

HOW ANIMALS SAVED THE PEOPLE

ANIMAL TALES FROM THE SOUTH

retold by J. J. Reneaux

illustrated by James Ransome

HarperCollinsPublishers

To the animals of the earth and the children who love them
—J.J.R.

In memory of the lively spirit of J. J. Reneaux. Thanks
for your wonderful stories. We'll all miss you.
—J.R.

The author extends many thanks to the following for their
assistance and creative support—James Ransome; Greg Keyes;
Charles Hudson; and
The "Rockin' Reinharts": Max, Tess, and Jack.

Watercolors were used for the full-color illustrations.
The text type is 14.5-point Aldine.

Printed in Hong Kong by South China Printing Company
(1988) Ltd.
All rights reserved.
www.harperchildrens.com

Library of Congress Cataloging-in-Publication Data
Reneaux, J. J., date.
How animals saved the people: animal tales from the South
/ retold by J. J. Reneaux; illustrated by James Ransome.
p. cm.
Summary: A collection of folktales from people in the Deep
South including Cajun, Creole, Native Americans, African
Americans, those of English as well as Scotch-Irish-German
traditions, and others living in Appalachia.
ISBN 0-688-16253-3 (trade) — ISBN 0-688-16254-1 (library)
1. Tales—Southern States.   [1. Folklore—Southern States.]
I. Ransome, James, ill.   II. Title.
PZ8.1.R278 Ho 2001   398.2'0975'0452—dc21
[E]   99-52379

1 2 3 4 5 6 7 8 9 10
❖
First Edition

Contents

Introduction

Down South people have always loved a good story, and nowhere in the United States is storytelling more alive. Whether it's gossip on the porch, ghost stories at camp-outs, or folktales at bedtime, the gift of gab just comes natural to most Southerners.

Maybe it's because our great-great-great-great-grandparents came from places where people loved to tell stories too. Places like Ireland, where folks still enjoy trying to best one another with the tallest tale or the funniest play on words. Places like West Africa, where storytellers use laughter to teach wisdom. Places like the South itself, where over forty Indigenous (Native American) tribes passed on their beliefs through myths for many thousands of years.

In the New World they all came together and their lives were changed forever. It wasn't long before the European, Indigenous, and African-American cultures began influencing one another. Though they must have seemed strange to one another at first, each knew sadness, laughter, fear, and hope—and they all loved good stories, especially stories about animals. These folktales had universal appeal, after all, and the animals in them really did act a whole lot like people!

While each group told stories for entertainment and to pass on lessons in living, there were also other reasons for telling animal stories. European immigrant frontier families, for instance, must have felt isolated and afraid in the wilderness. Funny hunting stories and tall tales in which animals were either loyal friends or conquered foes may have helped them to feel stronger.

For African-American slaves, animal stories also provided a way to communicate forbidden ideas. Denied every basic right and living in horrible conditions, these slaves must have taken courage in stories in which smaller and weaker critters outsmarted bigger, more powerful varmints. Through these stories they could safely communicate their longing for justice and freedom. It would have been very dangerous for slaves to talk about these ideas in everyday conversation, but they could express their thoughts through animal characters in stories.

To the Indigenous peoples of North America, animals *were* people and were regarded with respect. They felt a special kinship with them, naming their clans for animals like the deer and bear. With the arrival of the Europeans and their African slaves, many Indigenous peoples perished from disease and warfare. The survivors saw their ways of life disappearing. More and more, stories became a way to keep their history, traditions, and pride alive as they were forced from their ancient lands and sent far away.

My own European, African, and Indigenous ancestors have spiced up my family's storytelling traditions like hot pepper sprinkled in a gumbo, and animal stories were among the first tales I heard and retold. Those bodacious critter folks kept me out of trouble more than a few times. But their value reaches far beyond childhood lessons. They have much to teach us about who we are as Americans and as human beings. Through them we can laugh at our own silly fears and foolishness as they gently remind us that we are all more alike than we are different.

So, I invite you to read and enjoy. When you are done, you can honor the animals and their gifts to us by retelling these stories to your family and friends.

—J. J. Reneaux

The GollyWhumper
APPALACHIAN

DOWN IN A DEEP SHADY HOLLER, where a shining mountain river comes busting through the gorge, old Aunt Molly lived alone in a little cabin in the pines. Her wrinkly-crinkly blue eyes had a merry twinkle, and laughter was never far from her heart. Aunt Molly worked hard to make a living, but sometimes it seemed she grew more stones than cabbages. Still, the old woman didn't begrudge ary a soul their good fortune, not even her rich miserly neighbor who lived down the dirt road.

She didn't mind that the ol' man was stingy, but the mean way he treated the mountain critters made her mad enough to spit. That rich farmer had got himself a snarling guard dog and set sharp-toothed traps all about his garden. The wild animals had pert near been scared off the mountain. Aunt Molly shook her head at such goin's on. What goes around, comes around, she thought. Someday that rich fella might just wish he'd treated the critters better.

Now one day Aunt Molly was fixing to get herself a drink of water from her cedar bucket when she dropped her good dipper gourd and broke a hole in it. "Goodness, gracious," she says, "now what am I goin' to do? There is nary a dry gourd about the place." The old woman went out behind the house where she grew gourd vines around a little tree. There was only one green gourd on the vine.

Druther not pick a green gourd, she thought. Folks say a green gourd'll witch ye. Well, I reckon I got to have me a dipping gourd. This big'n here will do fine.

The old woman started into pulling on the gourd. She pulled and pulled until, at last, the gourd popped off the vine. GOLLY-WHUMP!

Aunt Molly toted the gourd into the cabin and set it up on the fireboard to dry. She settled into her rocking chair and took up her knitting. Suddenly that big green gourd came rolling off the fireboard and hit the floor. GOLLYWHUMP!

"What in the tarnation?" The old lady got up to set the gourd back on the fireboard, and propped a big stick of kindling against it. "Now you just stay put right there, Mr. Gourd," she fussed, and went back to her knitting.

She had no more settled into her rocking chair when that gourd started to twitching and whumping around on the fireboard. GOLLYWHUMP! It smashed the clock to smithereens. The gourd bumped down to the cabin floor and started whumping away at everything in sight.

GOLLYWHUMP-WHUMP-WHUMP! Her chamber pot went flying, her best quilt ripped apart, fruit jars and dishes were smashing all over the place, and the spinning wheel was whumped to splinters. Then the big green gourd started chasing the old woman round and round that tore-up cabin.

"Oh, Law," Aunt Molly hollered at the top of her lungs, "I got a big green witchy GollyWhumper of a gourd after me!"

She headed for the door and near about escaped. But just as she was running out of the house, the gourd caught up with her. GOLLYWHUMP-WHUMP-WHUMP! It whumped her right smack on her bottom. The poor old woman howled like a beat dog as she was sent sailing through the air and out over the porch. She landed smack dab in the middle of the cabbage patch with a big THUMP!

Aunt Molly lit out down the dirt road toward her neighbor's house, but no matter how fast she ran, the gourd caught up with her. GOLLYWHUMP-WHUMP-WHUMP! It smacked her hard upside her tailfeathers.

"Oh, Law," she hollered, "I got to get shed of that big green GollyWhumper of a witchy gourd 'fore it whumps me to death!"

That old woman ran and ran until she came upon Groundhog sitting out in front of his house. "What's the matter, ol' Granny?" said he. "Looks like you runnin' from trouble!"

"Oh, Law," she squalled, "I got a big green GollyWhumper chasin' me!"

"Well, you just come on into my house. You always been good to us animals. Why, I'll fix that GollyWhumper!" The old woman ducked into Groundhog's house and hid behind the door.

That GollyWhumper came traveling up and rolled right inside the house. Groundhog jumped on the gourd and held on for dear life. GOLLYWHUMP-WHUMP-WHUMP! The gourd whumped him upside the head, knocked him back into a somersault, and sent him crashing into the old lady.

"Oo-oo-ooh, Law," she hollered. "Run for your life!"

Aunt Molly ran out the door, lickety-split, fast as her old legs would carry her. Pretty soon she saw Pant'er stretched out in front of his house. Pant'er raised up and eyed the old woman. "What'cha runnin' from, Granny? Got yourself some kind of trouble?"

"Got a big green GollyWhumper of a witchy gourd after me," she huffed. "It's about to whump me to pieces!"

"You always been good to us critters," said Pant'er. "Jump into my house. I'll take care of that GollyWhumper for ye!"

Aunt Molly leaped into Pant'er's house and hid behind the door. The GollyWhumper flew right in behind her. Pant'er tore into that

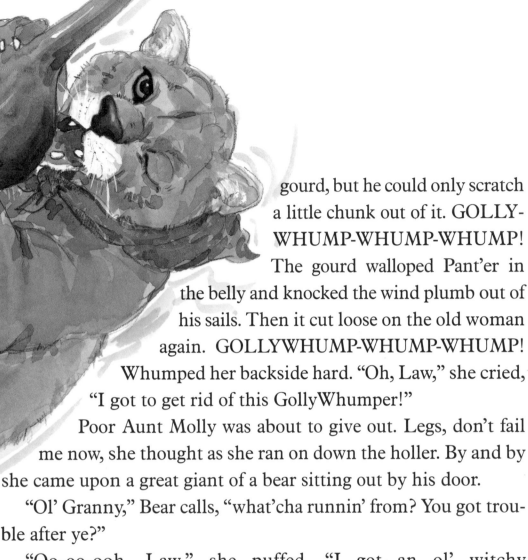

gourd, but he could only scratch a little chunk out of it. GOLLY-WHUMP-WHUMP-WHUMP! The gourd walloped Pant'er in the belly and knocked the wind plumb out of his sails. Then it cut loose on the old woman again. GOLLYWHUMP-WHUMP-WHUMP! Whumped her backside hard. "Oh, Law," she cried, "I got to get rid of this GollyWhumper!"

Poor Aunt Molly was about to give out. Legs, don't fail me now, she thought as she ran on down the holler. By and by she came upon a great giant of a bear sitting out by his door.

"Ol' Granny," Bear calls, "what'cha runnin' from? You got trouble after ye?"

"Oo-oo-ooh, Law," she puffed. "I got an ol' witchy GollyWhumper of a big green gourd after me. It's about to whump me to death. I have run and hid behind every blame door down the holler! Look out, yonder it comes again!"

"You always been good to the wild things," says Bear. "Quick, run in my house. I'll fix that GollyWhumper!"

Aunt Molly ran and hid behind the door, but ol' Bear jumped in and nosed her into the clothes closet. "You stay put over there, ol' woman," says he, "and leave everything to me." Bear hid behind the front door just in the nick of time.

Suddenly the GollyWhumper came whizzing in like a cannon shot, screeched to a halt, turned back behind the door, and aimed at Bear. But before it could whump ary a thing, Bear reared up, scooted around, and sat down hard on it with all his might. SSSQUASSSHHH!

Bear squeezed all the stuffins out of that gourd! All that was left of that big green Golly-Whumper was a heap of nasty crumbs.

Aunt Molly was so happy to be set free from the Golly-Whumper, she clapped and whooped and laughed and hollered. She got out a broom and swept the mess of GollyWhumper into the fireplace and burned it to ashes. "I surely am obliged to you and all them critters," she said. "Ain't there a little somethin' I can do for ye?"

"Well," says Bear, "it's been an awful long time since I had me a taste of honey. That rich ol' miser man who lives down the road is pretty rough on the critters, so I don't get out much these days to look for any wild honey. I would purely love a taste."

Aunt Molly had an idea. "Follow me," she says. Back up the holler they went to Pant'er's house. Poor ol' Pant'er was all bruised and sore. "Pant'er, you did your part to help me with that ol' GollyWhumper," she said. "Now, what can I do for ye?"

Pant'er studied on it. "Reckon could I have a taste of meat?" he asked. "It's been ever so long since I've had me a good meal. Huntin' ain't been no blame good lately, what with that ol' miser man's snarlin' dog chasin' away all the game."

Aunt Molly smiled. "Don't you fret another minute," she says. "I believe we might just find you a nice smoked ham. You just come on with Bear and me." They all set out walking to Groundhog's house. They found the poor feller sitting in a daze with a knot on his head and a swolled-up nose.

"Groundhog, you are a good friend to stick up for me," said the old woman. "I am much obliged. Now, tell me, what can I do for ye?"

Groundhog rubbed his swollen snout. "Well, a mess of turnips 'ould be jest fine. I ain't had no good eatin' from the garden lately, what with that ol' miser man's bitin' traps."

"Follow me," says the old woman, and took them back down the road to the rich man's house. "Now, boys, the way I figger it, you done my neighbor a good turn. He just don't know it yet. His dog and traps weren't no match against that big green witchy gourd. Why, that GollyWhumper would have whumped his fine farm to pieces."

Aunt Molly grinned, and her wrinkly-crinkly eyes twinkled. "It's only right that you fellers get a reward for savin' his farm. Now, don't worry about a thing. I got a plan, and as for that ol' miser man, I'll explain it all to him later."

Aunt Molly knew her rich neighbor had gone away to town, leaving his mean ol' dog to guard the place. "You'ns just wait over in them bushes," she said. The animals hid themselves, and the old woman went to the split-rail fence. She heaved up the heavy top

rail. Then she put her fingers to her mouth and gave out a keen whistle. TOO-WHEEE!

Hound Dog came running. When he saw a stranger at his fence and smelled the scent of wild varmints, he set up a loud ruckus, baying and barking and snapping and growling. WOO-WOO-WOO-WOO-WOO AH-WO-O-O! Hound Dog charged at that fence and stuck his slobbery chops right under that raised rail. Quick as a wink, Aunt Molly dropped the rail and pinned the dog down tight. Hound Dog was stuck in her trap and couldn't do a thing except whine like a fretful baby.

The old woman heisted up her skirts and eased her old bones over the fence. Groundhog shimmied through a little gap in the rails while Bear humped himself over. Pant'er leaped over the fence, easy as pie. They all scattered about to get their reward. Bear found a big jar of sourwood honey. Pant'er found a smoked ham hanging from the rafters and clawed it down. The old woman gave Groundhog a pokey sack, and he filled it to busting with garden turnips.

All the animals went back home feeling good that they had helped their neighbors and earned a fine reward. Aunt Molly told that ol' miser man all about the GollyWhumper and how the critters had rescued her and surely saved his farm. Her rich neighbor was ashamed of his mean, stingy ways. He took up his traps, hushed his dog with a ham bone, and gave the old woman enough dipping gourds to last her from now to forever.

Aunt Molly was satisfied. She had the river to sing her to sleep, the wild things to watch over her, the friendship of a neighbor, and she never had to pick another big green GollyWhumper of a witchy gourd ever again.

15

How Miz Gator Lost Her Pea-Green Suit

African-American

BACK IN THE OLDEN DAYS, Miz Gator loved dressing up in her beautiful, smooth-as-silk, pea-green suit and showing it off to all the other critters. Like a queen on her throne, she'd stretch out on the Mississippi River bank and admire the way her suit glowed in the morning sunshine. She was so full of herself that she never saw past the end of her own smooth-as-silk, pea-green tail.

One day as she was lying in the sun, that ol' rascal Br'er Rabbit came bounding down the riverbank in a great hurry. THUMPITY-THUMPITY-THUMPITY-THUMP! When he saw Miz Gator sunning herself, he stopped cold in his tracks. He knew he best not get too close to her snout.

Miz Gator lazily opened her eyes. "Why, Br'er Rabbit, I'm proud to see you. It's been quite a spell since I had a visit from you or any of your kinfolk. Y'all know how much I enjoy your company," she said with a snap of her big teeth.

"Well, it's nice to see you, too, Miz Gator," Br'er Rabbit said, keeping his distance. "There's nothin' better I'd love to do than visit, but I've just met up with trouble and I'm in a hurry to get back to my hole."

"What? You met up with Trouble? Now, just who is this Trouble fella?" she demanded. "Is he important?"

Br'er Rabbit sat back on his haunches and slyly eyed the alligator. "Important? Why, Mr. Trouble gets more attention than anything. Everybody knows Trouble. You mean to tell me that you have never met up with Trouble? You? The Queen of the Mississippi in your fine, smooth-as-silk, pea-green suit? Miz Gator, I can't believe my ears."

Miz Gator was horrified. Everybody but her knew Trouble! Why, all the critters must be laughing at her behind her back. Why hadn't Trouble come to call on her? "Now, Br'er Rabbit, you just go tell Mr. Trouble to come on by my place," she huffed. "It just ain't right for him to snub me that way."

"Now, don't you worry, Miz Gator," said Br'er Rabbit. "Why, I would be glad to introduce you to Trouble. All you got to do is meet me in the middle of Man's dried-up cornfield at high noon today. I guarantee, you are goin' to meet up with Trouble."

"Why, I can't thank you enough, Br'er Rabbit," Miz Gator exclaimed. "Just think, most folks say you always got a trick up your sleeve, but I can see that's just gossip."

Miz Gator was about to bust with excitement as she hurried back to her hole to get fixed up. She was polishing her smooth-as-silk, pea-green suit when her little ol' gator babies came home.

"Mama, Mama," they cried, "where you goin'?"

"Well, I'm goin' to meet up with Mr. Trouble, that's where I'm goin'," she says. "He is a mighty important fella. Br'er Rabbit is goin' to personally introduce me."

The gator babies didn't want to be left at home. They wanted to meet Trouble, too. Those children started into whining and crying. "Oh, Mama, we wanna go. Please, Mama, we wanna go. Take us with you, do, Mama, do!"

Miz Gator couldn't stand all the racket. "Well, all right then," she snapped, "but y'all better mind your manners. Now, hurry up and polish your pea-green suits."

Miz Gator proudly led her children up the riverbank to the cornfield. They crept into Man's field, their smooth-as-silk, pea-green suits glowing in the bright sun.

Sure enough, they found Br'er Rabbit sitting on a stump in the middle of that dried-up cornfield, waiting for them with the patience of a buzzard. "My, my," he says, "Miz Gator, you and your babies is a sight to see. Now, y'all just wait right here and keep lookin' for Mr. Trouble. He'll be comin' right along."

With that, Br'er Rabbit bounded away. When he was out of sight, he broke off some dried cornstalks and lit them for a torch. Then that rascal carried the torch and ran round and round in a circle, setting the field on fire. Soon those poor gators were caught in a burning ring of fire. The gator children looked up at the sky and saw billowing smoke. They had never seen smoke or fire

before. "Ooh, look, Mama, look!" The children giggled. "What's that funny-lookin' stuff in the sky? Reckon that's Mr. Trouble?"

"Hush, babies," says Miz Gator. "Quit that laughin'. Mr. Trouble might hear y'all."

Just then the gators saw something orange and red and golden dancing through the dry cornstalks. They could feel heat leaping toward them. "Ooh, look, Mama, look!" the children cried. "Trouble is pretty, but Trouble sure is hot!"

"Shhh!" Miz Gator hissed. "Don't be talkin' 'bout Trouble that way. It ain't polite!"

The gators watched as the flames burned closer and closer. They began to sweat in their smooth-as-silk, pea-green suits. Finally, Miz Gator and her children couldn't bear the heat any longer. "Quick, babies, follow me. We got to get out of this field right now!" Miz Gator bellowed. "We don't want to meet up with Trouble after all!"

HWEESH, HWEESH, HWEESH! The gators ran through the burning ring of fire fast as their short legs could carry them, down to the Mississippi River, and plunged their smoking suits into the cool water. SPLISH, SPLASH, HISSSSS! SPLISH, SPLASH, HISSSSS! SPLISH, SPLASH, HISSSSS! AAAAAAAHHHHHHH!

When Miz Gator and her children got back to their hole, they looked at one another and started crying great big alligator tears. Their beautiful, smooth-as-silk, pea-green suits were ruined, scorched into a tough hide, greenish brown like the Mississippi, and lumpy as the muddy riverbank. Miz Gator and her kinfolk lost their smooth-as-silk, pea-green suits forever. But they did find out the truth about Trouble, and now you know it too:

If you look for Trouble, then Trouble you will find,
Never trouble Trouble, just let it pass on by!

How the Bear People Lost Fire
ALABAMA—INDIGENOUS (NATIVE AMERICAN)

AFTER THE HUMAN PEOPLE were created and began to walk about, they soon became very hungry. There were wild foods to eat in the warm months, but in the cold winter their bellies often grumbled. Hunting was of little use to them, for they had no way to cook game. The Human people did not yet possess Fire. In those days, the Bear people were the Keepers of Fire. Chief Bear did not want to share Fire with the two-legged newcomers, so he and his people carried it with them everywhere they went.

Once the Bear people were hungry. As they went out in search of food, they came upon a wood filled with good acorns. Chief Bear set Fire on the ground and commanded Hunter Bear to tend it. "You feed Fire," he growled. "I am Chief and I am hungry." The chief went quickly into the wood, leaving Hunter Bear to tend Fire.

Hunter Bear began to think of the delicious acorns lying thick upon the ground, and his stomach rumbled with hunger. Just then, Hunter Bear saw Old Woman Bear walking with a basket to the wood to gather acorns. "You there, Old Woman, it is your turn to feed Fire," he demanded. "A hunter must eat to keep up his strength."

Old Woman Bear waited patiently beside the fire. I am feeding Fire, she thought, but I am forgotten. Nobody brings me acorns so that I may eat. Old Woman Bear saw Young Bear heading toward the wood. "Listen to me," she ordered. "I am old and I am hungry. I must go and gather my own acorns or I will surely starve. Stay here and do not forget to feed Fire."

Young Bear fed Fire with interest for a while, but then he grew bored and hungry. "Why should everyone else eat acorns while I feed Fire? No one will know if I go and gather acorns. I am small, and it will not take long for me to eat my fill. I will hurry back to Fire before Old Woman Bear returns." Young Bear left Fire and ran into the wood to eat acorns.

Fire burned lower and lower until it was only a weak flame licking at the coals. "Feed me," Fire called. The Bears were deep in the wood and did not hear Fire. "Feed me," Fire cried again and again. Fire was almost extinguished. A thin wisp of smoke coiled up into the air. Once more, Fire called out with its last bit of strength, "Feed me!"

A small band of the new Human people were passing by and heard the call. They came to the place where Fire was dying. "Feed me!" Fire whispered. "If you give me sticks to burn, it will be a good thing. I will warm you on cold nights. I will give you light and protect you in the dark of night. If you take care of me, you will have many good things to eat in all the seasons."

The Human people took a stick from the North and fed it to Fire. They took a second stick from the West and gave it to Fire. From the South they took a stick and laid it on Fire. In the East they found another stick and offered it to Fire. A bright flame

licked the wood hungrily, and Fire blazed up hot and strong.

Suddenly the Human people heard the Bear people coming. Young Bear came running up first and saw the Humans feeding Fire. "What are you doing?" he cried. "Fire belongs to the Bears!"

Fire grew stronger. "The Bear people left me to starve," it crackled. "I do not know you any longer."

Next came Old Woman Bear carrying a basket full of acorns. She was angry to see the Humans tending Fire. "Why do you feed the flames?" she demanded. "Fire belongs to the Bear people."

Fire rose higher. "You left me alone to starve," it sizzled. "I do not know the Bear people anymore."

Just then, Hunter Bear sprinted from the wood. "Stop feeding Fire," he growled. "Fire belongs to the Bear people."

Fire burned brighter. "The Bear people forgot me. They left me to starve," it popped. "I do not know them anymore."

Suddenly, a roar rang out as Chief Bear bolted from the wood. "Go away, Human people! Fire belongs to the Bears."

Fire flamed up red-hot. "The Bear people left me alone to starve and die," it blazed. "The Human people saved my life, and now I am their friend. They will never forget Fire. They will always need me. I will live with the Humans now. I do not know the Bear people any longer."

Fire stayed with the Human people and never returned to live with the Bears. The Humans always remembered to feed Fire and they received many gifts in return. Fire gave them warmth, light, and protection, and from that time on they had many good things to eat throughout all the seasons.

Bouki and Lapin Divide the Crops
CREOLE

IT WAS SPRING AND TIME TO plant a crop, but Trouble was visiting the land. If it wasn't drought, it was flood. All the critters were short on luck, but Bouki the Wolf whined and complained more than anybody.

One day Lapin the Rabbit heard his neighbor Bouki fussing over the weather and hard times. "*Mon ami,* worry less and think more," says the clever Lapin. "We got to use our heads and outsmart Trouble. Just think how rich we are goin' to be if we farm together. We can each do our part. We will each buy half the seeds, do half the work, and then we will split the money from the crop fifty-fifty."

Bouki liked the idea of making money, for he was a greedy fellow, but he didn't trust anybody, especially not Lapin. "Oh, I know all about your tricky ways, Rabbit." Bouki frowns. "You got to get up pretty early to pull the wool over my eyes. Me, I got a better idea. You buy the seed, and I'll do all the plowin' and plantin'. We

29

sure will split that crop. You take what's on top, and me, I'll take what is on the bottom. Nobody cheats Bouki!"

Lapin grinned from ear to ear. "Well, if that is the way you want it, that is the way you are goin' to get it. It is too bad you don't trust your neighbor, but you are much smarter than me. We will divide the crop just as you say. You plow the field and I'll bring the seed."

Before long Bouki had plowed the rich black Delta earth. Lapin bought the seeds and Bouki planted them. "Now, Bouki, I am goin' to give you one more chance. Are you sure you don't want to split the crop fifty-fifty?" asks Lapin.

"I know what you're up to, Lapin," Bouki says, scowling. "No, I don't want to split the money from the whole crop. I just want the half what grows below the ground. That way you rabbits can't eat all the best pickin's from the top before I get my half. Ha, ha, ha! Thought ya tricked me, didn't ya?"

Every day Lapin came to look at their crop, but Bouki wasn't interested. After all, his half of the crop was out of sight, below the ground. At last the crop was ready to be harvested and Bouki discovered that they had grown only crops that grow above the ground—melons, corn, beans, and cabbages.

When Bouki saw that his share of the crop was only roots, he pitched a big fit, stomping and hollering, "ROOTS? I GOT NOTHIN' BUT ROOTS! Lapin, you tricked me. Why you're nothin' but a low-down-long-ear'd cheat of a rabbit!"

"*Mon ami,* do you not remember?" asked Lapin. "I gave you your choice. You got just what you asked for. But don't worry, all is not lost, you can feed the roots to your cows. Besides, there's always next year! Surely next spring your luck will change."

The next spring Bouki decided he would outsmart Lapin and get even. "This year I am goin' to get all the crop that grows above the ground. I'll teach you a thing or two for true!" bragged the wolf.

"Pardnah, why you want to be that way?" asks Lapin. "We are neighbors, why not share the money from the crop?"

"No! I want the top part of the crop," Bouki demanded.

"C'est bon," says Lapin. "We will do as you wish."

Once again Lapin bought the seed and Bouki plowed and planted. "That Lapin thinks he is so smart"—the wolf laughed wickedly—"but this year he's gettin' nothin' but roots! No rabbit is goin' to outsmart a wolf!"

At last it was time to harvest the crop. That's when Bouki discovered they had planted only root crops that grow below the ground—potatoes, turnips, peanuts, and carrots.

Bouki's eyes nearly popped out of his head.

"I GOT NOTHIN' BUT STEMS AND VINES!" the wolf cried. "Lapin, you are a no-good-double-crossin' snip-tail! Why, you never could have tricked me if it wasn't for my bad luck!"

Lapin only grinned and shook his head. "*Mon ami*, sometimes we make our luck. You tricked yourself out of a crop two years runnin', just 'cause you would not trust your neighbor. Besides, your luck is not all bad. There is one thing growing above the ground—gourd vines. You cannot eat them, but you will have plenty of dipper gourds, I guarantee!"

Waiting for BooZoo
AFRICAN-AMERICAN

ONE STORMY SUMMER EVENING, when distant thunder rumbled and rain tapped on the tin roof, some old-timers sat around a country store, spinning tales of a big lonesome haunted house. For fifty years a monster of a black cat called BooZoo had witched that house with a horrible spell. Rewards had been offered, but nobody had ever had the courage to face that dreadful haint down and break the power of its spell. The old men spat in the spittoon and agreed: There wasn't a soul around brave enough to stay in that haunted house all night and wait for BooZoo to come.

A young stranger in the store happened to overhear their stories and started laughing at the old men. "Y'all are scared of a cat? Why, there ain't no such thing as haints." The stranger spat. "If there was, I'd just go on up there to that big house and whup that BooZoo from tooth to toenail!"

"Well, then, young fella, why don't you just go find out for yo'-self?" one old toothless man said, grinning. All the men nodded in

35

agreement. "Yes, sir, that's right," the old-timer went on. "All you got to do is spend the night in the house and wait for BooZoo to come. If you face that witchy cat down and break his spell, that ol' man that owns the house is gonna pay you a thousand dollars."

The stranger sneered at the old men. "I ain't scared of nothin'!" he bragged. "Just give me a hunk of fryin' meat and a skillet and point me in the right direction. Y'all best not be lyin' 'bout that thousand dollars, 'cause I'll be here in the mornin' to collect my reward." The stranger got a hunk of ham and a skillet and off he went to the haunted house.

He found the big old abandoned place all boarded up and hung with cobwebs. He pulled off some boards and went inside. Taking a match and candle from his coat pocket, he lit the candle and peered into the shadows. In the dim light he saw a fireplace, neatly stacked with dry firewood.

"Well, I reckon somebody done left this firewood here a long time ago," he mumbled as he lit a fire. "Good thing, too, judgin' by that lightnin' flashin' outside. Looks like a real thunder boomer is brewin'. Well, I'll be dry tonight and rich in the morning! Now, for a little supper."

The young man built a fire and soon had a glowing bed of red-hot coals. He put the skillet on the coals, threw the ham into the frying pan, and sat down to cook his supper. The meat sizzled and the grease popped. The wind moaned and blew cold drops of rain down the chimney into the fire. SIZZLE, POP! WHOOOOO, HISSSSS!

Suddenly the door of the haunted house opened. C-R-E-A-K. A black cat came walking in, sat down on its haunches, and stared at the fella through slitty green eyes. The cat began to yowl:

36

"Yeee-ooo-www!
BooZoo is comin', better run for your life,
He's a giant black cat, teeth sharp as a knife!
Mister, are you crazy, are you some
    kind of fool,
Is you gonna be here when BooZoo come
    to get you?"

An icy chill ran down the young man's spine, but talkin' cat or not, he was determined to get that reward money. He watched the cat out of the corner of his eye, kept right on frying that ham, and said weakly,

"I m-made a bet and I'm sticking to it,
I'll be a rich man if I can d-do it,
I ain't gonna scat, I ain't gonna run,
Y-yeah, I'll be here when B-BooZoo comes!"

The cat sat still as stone, watching the fellow tend his supper. The meat sizzled, the grease popped, the wind moaned, and the rain hissed. SIZZLE, POP! WHOOOOO, HISSSSS!

Just then the stranger heard the door open again. C-R-E-A-K. A second black cat, the size of a lion, came slinking into the room, sat on its haunches, glared at the young man with glittery green eyes, and howled,

"Yeee-ooo-www!
BooZoo is comin', better run for your life,
He's a giant black cat, teeth sharp as a knife!
Mister, are you crazy, are you some kind of fool,
Is you gonna be here when BooZoo come to get you?"

37

The fellow gulped hard and kept right on frying his ham. He was trembling so hard, he could barely answer:

"I m-made a bet, and I'm sticking to it,
I'll be a rich man if I can d-d-do it!
I ain't gonna scat, I ain't gonna run,
Y-Y-Yeah, I'll be here when B-B-BooZoo comes!"

The two cats sat silent and unblinking as the man tended his supper. The meat sizzled, the grease popped, the wind moaned, and the rain hissed. SIZZLE, POP! WHOOOOO, HISSSSS!

All of a sudden, the door opened a third time. C-R-E-A-K. A bolt of lightning lit up the beast that stood in the doorway. A gigantic black cat, big as a grizzly bear, pounced into the room, swishing its long bushy tail. Its green glassy eyes were shining as it crept up to the fire.

The young man backed away, his legs trembling like jelly, his eyes round as supper plates. In the blink of an eye, the monster cat snagged the burning-hot meat from the frying pan and swallowed it whole, before lifting the sizzling skillet and pouring the popping grease down his gullet. Then, reaching behind, the cat hooked its long bushy tail and wiped its greasy mouth.

The monster grinned wickedly, arched its back, stretched its claws, and started to yowl:

"Yeee-ooo-www, yeee-ooo-www, yeee-ooo-www!
BooZoo is comin', better run for your life,
He's a giant black cat, teeth sharp as a knife!
Mister, are you crazy, are you some kind of fool,
Is you gonna be here when BooZoo come to get you?"

The young man's eyes bulged, and his hair stood up on his head. "A-Ain't YOU BooZoo?" he chattered.

The huge cat grinned wickedly. "No," he growled, *"I ain't BooZoo. He's BIGGER than me. Is you gonna be here when BooZoo come to get you?"*

"N-O-O-O-O-O!" the fellow screeched. "IF Y-Y-YOU AIN'T B-B-BOOZOO, I AIN'T GONNA B-BE HERE WHEN B-B-BOOZOO COMES!"

SHO-O-O-M! That young man's feet took off ahead of the rest of him, and he went streaking out the door like greased lightnin', never to be seen again. He is long gone now, but that thousand-dollar reward is still waiting for a brave soul like you, to wait for BooZoo, and break his spell on that haunted house, once and for all.

The Poopampareno
DEEP SOUTH—ENGLISH, SCOTS-IRISH, AND GERMAN

ON A CRISP FALL NIGHT IN Deep East Texas, when the fox hunters gather about the fire to tell old stories, you may hear a strange and frightening tale. Pointing into the smoky darkness, they will show you the thicket where the scaly-skinned Thing was last seen, shaking his wild pine-needle mane and grinding his teeth, sharp as a crosscut saw. Then, as you shiver in the suddenly chilly night, the old men will lean into the firelight and tell you the story of the dreadful Poopampareno.

There was once an old hermit who lived down in the thick piney woods of Deep East Texas. Most folks called him Old Man McCann, and seeing as how he never had a good word to say about anything, they left him alone to his solitary ways. Old Man McCann was one cranky fusspot of a fellow who didn't have any friends—leastways, not any human friends.

What the hermit did have was Fido and T-bone, two of the finest hunting dogs to be found anywhere in the South. Fido's eyes

41

had grown dim with age, but he could still sniff out the wiliest fox in the black of night and bay as loud as a train whistle. T-bone was quick as a rabbit and eager as a frisky pup for the thrill of the hunt.

One fall day Old Man McCann thought he would go into the woods and cut trees for railroad ties. "My pockets are empty, boys," he told the dogs. "If I'm goin' to keep you dogs in milk and corn bread, I best get to work." The hermit penned up his faithful hounds out back. Fido howled like his old heart was breaking, while T-bone yelped to follow his master.

"Now, hush, puppies," says McCann. "I'll be back at dark. I ain't a-goin' huntin' without my good dogs—I am just goin' to go cut some cross ties. I got to earn us a livin'!"

The old man set a big pan of milk inside the pen. "This ought to hold ya 'til I can get some more cornmeal. Now, quit frettin' so. All that talk lately about a boogeyman with big ol' sawteeth is plumb nonsense. Ain't no such thing as a Poopampareno. Just watch that pan of milk. Long as it's white, you'll know I'm safe."

The old hermit loaded his wagon and hitched up his mule. He turned the rig toward the woods, leaving Fido and T-bone wailing and barking in their pen.

McCann stopped occasionally to cut timber with his cross-blade saw, moving his rig deeper and deeper into the woods. The shadows were long by the time he came to a dark thicket. Well, it's gettin' late, he thought. I'll just cut one more tree and load up all that cut timber on my way back.

McCann was busy sawing when he heard a strange buzzing sound coming from the thicket. He stopped working and listened. ZZZH-ZZZAH, ZZZH-ZZZAH, ZZZH-ZZZAH. Hmm, he thought, must be some other feller cuttin' timber over yonder. He went back to sawing on the tree.

ZZZH-ZZZAH, ZZZH-ZZZAH, ZZZH-ZZZAH. There was that raspy buzzing again, louder than before, and closer. The hermit peered into the thicket and listened. The sound had stopped as suddenly as it had begun. The only movement he heard was the flapping of wings as birds flew from the thicket and scattered into the sky.

"Well, that feller sawin' over there must be a-trespassin', the way he is sneakin' around out in the thicket." Once again he put his saw to the tree and threw his back into the work.

Then came that buzzing again, louder than ever, from right behind him. ZZZH-ZZZAH, ZZZH-ZZZAH, ZZZH-ZZZAH. The old man wheeled around and felt the hair on the back of his neck stand up. There, standing before him, was the ugliest Thing he had ever seen. He tried to holler out, but the words stuck in his throat.

"It's the Poo— It's the Pam— It's the Poopampareno!" he gasped.

Sure enough, it was that ol' piney-woods monster. Its hair was as bushy and green as pine needles, and its skin was as rough and scaly as tree bark. Worst of all were its pointy teeth, sharp and raspy as the blade of a crosscut saw. The Poopampareno grinned at the hermit and gnashed its sawteeth. ZZZH-ZZZAH, ZZZH-ZZZAH, ZZZH-ZZZAH!

Old Man McCann knew he didn't stand a chance against the creature. Some said the Poopampareno had only one weak spot—and that was right under its jaw. The hermit didn't aim to get close enough to those awful sawteeth to find out. Instead, he threw down his crosscut saw and ran like a deer through the woods. He spied a great old loblolly pine and leaped for his life, swinging himself up on a branch and climbing higher and higher until there was nothing but sky above him. He looked down at the monster and saw he was in big trouble. The Poopampareno grinned up at him and ground its awful teeth. ZZZH-ZZZAH, ZZZH-ZZZAH, ZZZH-ZZZAH!

As the old man watched in horror, the monster attacked the tree with its sharp sawteeth. Wood chips and sawdust flew. The only thing that could save him now was his good ol' dogs!

McCann took a shaky breath and tried to call his hounds:

"Here, Fido! Come, T-bone!
Hurry up, boys, I'm almost gone!
It's the Poo— It's the Pam— It's the Poopampareno!"

Back at the pen, the dogs had gone to sleep. Suddenly, T-bone whimpered and woke up trembling. Fido raised his head and looked around. His old eyes didn't see anything, but his keen nose smelled trouble. He went over to the pan of milk. It was still creamy white. The two dogs sat at attention in their pen, listening and waiting for their master to return.

Meanwhile, in the piney-wood thicket, their master was desperately clinging to a swaying pine branch. The tree was creaking and the monster was sawing. ZZZH-ZZZAH, ZZZH-ZZZAH, ZZZH-ZZZAH. The Poopampareno had already sawed the tree in half!

The old man took a deep breath and tried to yell, but his call was only a little louder:

"Here, Fido! Come, T-bone!
Hurry up, boys, I'm almost gone!
It's the Poo— It's the Pam— It's the Poopampareno!"

Old Fido and young T-bone trotted nervously around the pen. The dogs couldn't hear their master's call, but they saw that the pan of milk had turned bloodred. Old Man McCann was in danger! Fido growled mean and low as he sniffed the air for his master's scent. T-bone yelped and desperately clawed at the fence, trying to force his way out.

The old man knew he didn't have much time left. ZZZH-ZZZAH, ZZZH-ZZZAH, ZZZH-ZZZAH. The tree was nearly cut through. Anytime now it would come crashing down!

McCann knew it was do or die. He sucked in air until he thought his lungs would burst, and hollered out,

"Here, Fido! Come, T-bone!
Hurry up, boys, I'm almost gone!
It's the Poo— It's the Pam— It's the Poopampareno!"

His call shot through the air, ricocheting off trees, bouncing off red-clay hills, all the way to Fido and T-bone.

Now, nothing in the world can stop a good dog when its master is in danger. Those faithful hounds charged again and again, until at last they crashed over the fence, bringing the pen down behind them. Off they ran, T-bone barking furiously and Fido baying like a runaway train:

"Master, Master, we're comin' on strong,
Faster, faster, it won't be long!
Hang on tight, ol' McCann,
Your good dogs are runnin' just as quick as we can!"

Back in the piney woods, the grinning Poopampareno was now only one cut away from having its supper. ZZZH-ZZZAH, ZZZH-ZZZAH, ZZZH-ZZZAAAHHH! Then, all of a sudden, Fido and T-bone leaped from the thicket. ARHOO, ARHOOO, ARHOOOOO! The dogs were upon the monster before it could rip its buzzing sawteeth from the tree. They sank their fangs deep into the monster's soft weak spot, right under its jaw. And that was the end of the terrible Poopampareno.

Fido and T-bone proved once more that a good dog is man's best friend. That hermit surely believed it, and he was grateful forever more to his faithful hounds. Folks say that, from that time on, Old Man McCann never went anywhere without Fido and T-bone, and as far as anyone knows, they are still roaming the piney woods of Deep East Texas.

Buzzard and Chicken Hawk
CAJUN

ONE DAY M'SIEUR CARENCRO, the buzzard, was sitting on a fence post real patientlike, just waiting for something to drop dead so he could have his supper. He was so hungry, his poor little ol' buzzard cheeks were all sunk in and he barely had any meat left on his bones. M'sieur Carencro sighed sadly, wondering when his bad luck was going to change.

All of a sudden, who should come flapping up but Mangeur de Poulet, the chicken hawk.

"Hey, man, *Ça va?* How's things goin' with you, *pardnah?*" asked Chicken Hawk. "You sittin' there all hunched over and pitiful, like you got the blues."

Buzzard sighed. "Oh, *Ça va mal.* Things are not goin' good at all. I been sittin' here for days waiting for somethin' to drop dead so I can have my supper. But I tell you, there ain't nothin' falling out of the sky for me. I think I'm gonna starve."

"Aw, man, whatcha talkin' about?" asked know-it-all Chicken

Hawk. "What is the matter for you? Look here. You got eyes, you got wings, you got a beak. If you're hungry, get up and go hunt you up some good fresh meat. Go for it! You got to look out for Number One in this world, *mon ami.*"

M'sieur Carencro shook his head sadly. "*Non, non, non,* you don't understand. I am s'posed to wait for something to drop dead before I eat it. It's my job to help keep the world clean. That's just the way *Le Bon Dieu* made me."

Mangeur de Poulet jumped back and eyed Buzzard. "*Le Bon Dieu?* Aw, *non!* Don't waste your breath talkin' 'bout the Good God," he said. "Besides, even if there is a God, what makes you think He cares about whether an ol' buzzard like you gets supper? Man, you got to be like me. You want somethin'? Just grab it. All that matters is that you get it. Get it? Here, let ol' Chicken Hawk show you how to do that thang!"

With that, he leaped into the air and zoomed up into the sky like a rocket. His wings were flapping wildly, and he started showing off, doing fancy loop-de-loops and crazy figure eights.

All of a sudden, Mangeur de Poulet looked down and spied a little juicy rabbit sitting in front of the fence post, right under Buzzard's feet. Oowhee, he thought, now there's some good eatin'. Only thing a hawk likes better than chicken is a juicy little rabbit.

Mangeur de Poulet took dead aim. He meant to snatch that bunny and gobble it up. "Hey, man, watch this!" he hollered. Down he swooped, faster and faster. *Z-O-O-O-O-O-M!* But Mamselle Lapin the rabbit was smart-smart. She saw Chicken Hawk's shadow closing in on her and she froze still as stone. Then, at the last split second, she jumped down her rabbit hole just in the nick of time.

It was too late for Mangeur de Poulet. He tried to slam on the brakes, but he was speeding too fast. BOIINNNGGG! Chicken

Hawk crashed smack dab into the fence post! And down he dropped—THUNK—deader than the fence post itself, right under Buzzard's feet.

Buzzard looked down at dead Chicken Hawk under his feet. He looked up to heaven. Buzzard grinned real big and says, *"Merci*

beaucoup, mon Grand Bon Dieu! Good God Almighty, thank you!"
M'sieur Carencro hopped down from the fence, smacked his
lips, and says, "Suppertime!"

And so, *mon ami*, maybe it is better to be like the Buzzard: Be who you are, have faith, do your work, and surely, good things will come your way.

How Animals Saved the People
CHOCTAW—INDIGENOUS (NATIVE AMERICAN)

MANY YEARS AGO when Earth was young, there was a certain vine that grew in the warm, slow-flowing bayous in the land of the Chahta Oklah, the Choctaw people. Vine was beautiful but poisonous. She held no danger for animals, but to humans one drop of her poison was deadly. They swam and bathed in the bayou, never realizing the danger. As the people brushed against Vine, poison fell from her leaves onto their skin. Soon men, women, and children sickened and died. Fear and sorrow filled the hearts of the Choctaw people, for they did not know the cause of this strange sickness and they were powerless to cure it.

Vine did not wish the people any harm. How could she save the Chahta Oklah from her deadly poison? One day Vine sent a message by Wind to the animals: "Come quickly, friends. There is danger in the land. Your help is needed!"

Wind whispered the message to the animals in its path. All that heard her call were filled with curiosity, and they came by land and water and air to speak with Vine. Some creatures were dressed in soft feathers or rippling fur. Some buzzed on silver-veined wings; others scurried in hard, armored suits; still others hopped or swam or slithered in cool, scaly skins. Animals as far as the eye could see gathered before Vine and demanded to know the danger.

Vine raised her leafy arms and spoke: "*Halito,* my friends. Be still now and listen. The Chahta Oklah are in danger. The people are new to this land and do not know me. They touch my leaves, and my poison makes them sicken and die. I do not wish them harmed. Help me, friends. Help me to save the Choctaw people!"

Many of the animals began to complain. "Why should we help?" they asked in surprise. "We animals live with danger, sickness, and death, but do the people help us? The people are new, and they, too, must learn how to live in the Creator's world."

At this, most of the creatures left the meeting and hurried back to their homes. Only a few stayed behind. These animals talked it over among themselves and agreed to do whatever

they could to help the people. Vine was their friend, and they knew she was very wise. "We trust you," they said. "Tell us what we must do."

"Come closer, friends," Vine urged. "Have no fear. My poison is like water to you, and it will not harm you. Each of you can take a little of my poison. In that way none of us alone will destroy the people, and all of us together can help to save them. Touch my leaves, and I will give you a few drops to carry away." Clan by clan, the animals approached Vine to receive a share of her poison.

The snakes came first. Many of their kind had gone away, and only a few remained. Water Moccasin spoke for them, saying, "We snakes promise to do our best to help the two-legged ones. We will mark ourselves with colors and patterns, and we will shape our heads and our bodies so that they will know we are special among snakes. If Humans stumble among us, we will try to flee, or we will hiss and sound a warning with our rattles. We will not frighten or harm the people unless they frighten or harm us."

"You have spoken well and I have listened," said Vine. "Come now and help the people."

The snakes slithered forward. With swift, darting tongues, the snakes touched Vine and took a few drops of poison into their bodies. At once their heads and bodies began to twist into thicker shapes, and new patterns and colors decorated their skins as they slithered away.

Next came the spiders, lizards, and a small number of slippery-skinned water creatures. Spider spoke for them all, saying, "We, too, will do our best to help the people. We will mark ourselves with colors and designs to warn people of our danger. If the two-legged ones come near us, we will try to hide. We will defend ourselves only if the people frighten or harm us."

"Your words speak truth," said Vine. "Come forward to help the people."

The creatures crawled and hopped and swam to touch Vine. Scales, skin, and tentacles brushed against her leaves, taking a little of the poison, each one according to its size. Delicate designs and bright hues painted their bodies as the creatures hurried away to their homes.

Next came Bee with her relatives, the wasps and hornets. Bee spoke for her family and all the flying creatures: "We animals of the air will stripe and color ourselves to remind people to respect us," she hummed. "Our buzzing will be a warning for all to hear. If people come near us, we will fly away and try to avoid them. We will not frighten or hurt the people unless they frighten or hurt us."

"You have spoken well and I have heard you," Vine said, nodding. "Come now and help the people."

The creatures of the air flew to Vine and fluttered

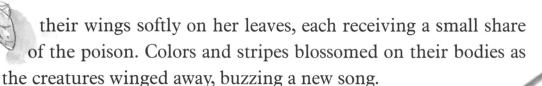

their wings softly on her leaves, each receiving a small share of the poison. Colors and stripes blossomed on their bodies as the creatures winged away, buzzing a new song.

The smallest creatures of the land had been waiting in line for a long time. Ant was the leader of these tiny, hard-shelled animals. Ant marched up impatiently. "We creatures of the soil will do our part," she said to Vine with dancing antennae. "We will take the last drop of poison from you, but we must be quick about it. There is work to do! The little animals promise to do their best to hide from the people. Our homes will be built within the earth. We will not harm the people. But if the two-legged ones step on our nests, we will defend our families!"

"Your words are wise," Vine said respectfully. "Bring your relatives to me and gather your share of my poison."

The creatures of the earth climbed Vine and tapped their antennae gently against her leaves. Small but strong, they took away the last drop of Vine's deadly poison and scurried away into the dark earth.

From that time on the people swam, fished, and bathed in the bayou without danger. After many seasons they came to understand how the animals took poison from Vine to save the Chahta Oklah. The people told the story to their children, and their children told their children, and on and on to this very time.

Listen and you may hear the Choctaw ancestors: Respect earth's creatures, and you will repay their gift and help to save the animals just as they once saved the people.

Glossary

In the pronunciation guide for words in other languages, capitalized syllables and words indicate where the accent is to be placed.

THE GOLLYWHUMPER

- **ary** any. "Ary a thing" is similar to saying "anything."
- **nary** not any; nothing, none
- **dipper gourd** a type of ladle used for drinking made from a dried long-neck gourd. Before mountain people had running water, they often kept a bucket of drinking water handy. When they were thirsty, they used their dipper to get a drink.
- **What in the tarnation?** an expression of surprise, anger, or fear heard especially in the South
- **Oh, Law** an expression meaning "Oh, Lord." Where people believe it is disrespectful to use "Lord" to express excitement, worry, fear, or anger, "Law" is often a word substituted to show manners and respect.
- **pert near** pretty near; almost

BOUKI AND LAPIN DIVIDE THE CROPS

- **Bouki** (BOO-kee) in Africa, a hyena. In the New World, since there were no hyenas, storytellers simply changed Bouki into a wolf. Also, in the Deep South, Bouki is a nickname for a person who is behaving stupidly.
- **Lapin** (lah-PAN, as in "can", but *n* is silent) French for "rabbit"; a trickster character from Cajun folklore

60

- **mon ami** (mohn ah-MEE) French for "my friend"
- **C'est bon** (say BOHN, as in "bone," but *n* is silent) French for "That's good" or "This is good"
- **pardnah** (pawd-NAH) buddy, pal
- **delta** the area of fertile farmland formed by silt that builds up at a river's mouth

WAITING FOR BOOZOO

- **haint** a haunt or a ghost

BUZZARD AND CHICKEN HAWK

- **M'sieur Carencro** (muh-SYOO KAH-rohn-kroh) French for "Mr. Buzzard"
- **Mangeur de Poulet** (MAHN-zhoor duh POO-lay) French for "Chicken Hawk"
- **Ça va** (sah VAH) French for "How's it going?"
- **Ça va mal** (sah vah MAHL) French for "It's not good; things are going bad."
- **non** (NON as in "bone", but *n* is silent) French for "no"
- **Le Bon Dieu** (luh bohn DYOO, middle syllable as in "bone" but *n* is silent) French for "The Good Lord"
- **Mamselle Lapin** (mahm-ZELL lah-PAN, as in "can", but *n* is silent) French for "Miss Rabbit"
- **Merci beaucoup, mon Grand Bon Dieu!** (mer-SEE boh-KOO, mohn GRON bohn DYOO) French for "Good God Almighty, thank you very much!"

HOW ANIMALS SAVED THE PEOPLE

- **Chahta Oklah** (CHAH-tah oke-LAH) Choctaw for "the Choctaw people"
- **halito** (hah-lee-TOH) Choctaw for "hello"

About These Stories

The GollyWhumper

This story is my adaptation of "The Green Gourd," which was collected by Richard Chase in the Appalachian Mountains and retold in *Grandfather Tales* (Boston: Houghton Mifflin, 1948). I have tried to reflect the language and humor of the Appalachian Mountains and the many communities in which I have lived and visited.

How Miz Gator Lost Her Pea-Green Suit

As a child, I heard this tale told as a Br'er Rabbit story. I have retold it here from memory as a pourquoi tale that explains the origin of alligator's dull, rough hide.

How the Bear People Lost Fire

My adaptation of this story is largely based upon research and articles by John R. Swanton, including "Myths and Tales of the Southeastern Indians" (*Bureau of American Ethnology Bulletin*, no. 88, Washington, D.C., 1931). Also, *The Southeastern Indians*, by Charles Hudson (Knoxville: University of Tennessee Press, 1976) was very important to my understanding of precontact Southeastern Indigenous cultures. A version also appears in *Native American Legends*, by George E. Lankford (Little Rock, Ark.: August House, 1987).

Bouki and Lapin Divide the Crops

My retelling is drawn from the Cajun/Creole culture of southeastern Texas and Louisiana, as well the work of Calvin Claudel in his article "Louisiana

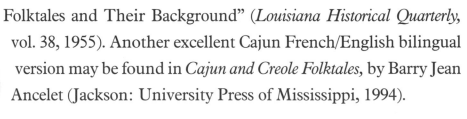

Folktales and Their Background" (*Louisiana Historical Quarterly*, vol. 38, 1955). Another excellent Cajun French/English bilingual version may be found in *Cajun and Creole Folktales*, by Barry Jean Ancelet (Jackson: University Press of Mississippi, 1994).

Waiting For BooZoo

I have modified for young readers a more mature version of "When Bozo Comes," found in *Storytellers: Folktales and Legends from the South*, edited by John A. Burrison (Athens: University of Georgia Press, 1989). The title name was changed to honor the coolest cat I've ever met, Creole Zydeco musician Boozoo Chavis.

The Poopampareno

I have heard several oral versions of this wonderful cross-cultural monster tale. Published sources include a variant in *A Treasury of Southern Folklore*, by B. A. Botkin (New York: Crown Publishers, 1949). My adaptation, which includes my own rhyming refrains, was strongly influenced by my daddy's boyhood hunting tales as well as the folklore of The Big Thicket (an expanse of dense forest located in East Texas, now a natural preserve).

Buzzard and Chicken Hawk

I heard this story many years ago from my neighbor, Mr. Laurence Molleré, and it has become one of my favorite stories to perform. It also appears in a slightly different version in my book *Cajun Folktales* (Little Rock, Ark.: August House, 1992) and in the collection *The Language of Literature* (Evanston, Ill.: McDougal and Littell, 1997).

How Animals Saved the People

My adapted retelling of this story was strongly influenced by my mother as well as friends of Choctaw heritage, including storyteller Tim Tingle and writer Greg Keyes. Published sources include "The Origin of Poison," which appears in Swanton and Lankford. I am also indebted to Indigenous publisher Gregg Howard of Speakers of the Earth for his assistance.

Dig a Little Deeper

More Animal Stories and Books

Bruchac, Joseph. *Keepers of the Animals.* Golden, Colo.: Fulcrum Publishing, 1989.

———. *The Great Ball Game: A Muskogee Story.* New York: Dial Books for Young Readers, 1994.

Cohn, Amy L. *From Sea to Shining Sea.* New York: Scholastic, 1993.

Doucet, Sharon Arms. *Why Lapin's Ears Are Long.* New York: Orchard Books, 1997.

Hamilton, Virginia. *A Ring of Tricksters.* New York: Blue Sky Press, 1997.

Holt, David, and Bill Mooney. *Ready-to-Tell Tales.* Little Rock, Ark.: August House, 1994.

Lester, Julius. *Further Tales of Uncle Remus.* New York: Dial Books for Young Readers, 1990.

McKissack, Patricia. *A Million Fish . . . More or Less.* New York: Alfred A. Knopf, 1992.

Parks, Van Dyke. *Jump! The Adventures of Brer Rabbit.* New York: Harcourt, Brace and Jovanovich, 1986.

Reneaux, J. J. *Cajun Folktales.* Little Rock, Ark.: August House, 1992.

———. *Why Alligator Hates Dog.* Little Rock, Ark.: August House, 1995.

Ross, Gayle. *How Turtle's Back Was Cracked: A Traditional Cherokee Tale.* New York: Dial Books for Young Readers, 1995.

Sloat, Terri. *Sody Sallyratus.* New York: Dutton Children's Books, 1997.

Van Laan, Nancy. *With a Whoop and a Holler.* New York: Atheneum Books for Young Readers, 1998.

Animal Stories and Songs for Listening
Audio Recordings

Bruchac, Joseph. *Keepers of the Animals.* Golden, Colo.: Fulcrum Publishing, 1989.

DeSpain, Pleasant. *Eleven Turtle Tales.* Little Rock, Ark.: August House, 1996.

Forest, Heather. *Tales around the Hearth.* Albany, N.Y.: A Gentle Wind, 1990.

Holt, David, and Bill Mooney. *Why Dog Chases the Cat.* Fairview, N.C.: High Windy, 1995.

Pirtle, Sarah. *Magical Earth.* Albany, N.Y.: A Gentle Wind, 1993.

Reneaux, J. J. *Cajun Folktales.* Little Rock, Ark.: August House, 1994.

———. *Wake Snake! Children's Stories and Songs of the South.* Little Rock, Ark.: August House, 1998.

Various Artists Compilation. *All about Animals.* Albany, N.Y.: A Gentle Wind, 1993.

Weiss, Jim. *Animal Tales.* Benicia, Calif.: Great Hall Productions, 1989.